# THIS BLOOMSBURY BOOK

## BELONGS TO

..............................................................

To my mother

First published in Great Britain in 2001 by Bloomsbury Publishing Plc
38 Soho Square, London, W1D 3HB
This paperback edition first published in 2002

Copyright © Michael Terry 2001
The moral right of the author/illustrator has been asserted

A CIP catalogue record of this book is available from the British Library
ISBN 0 7475 5534 6

Designed by Sarah Hodder
Printed in Hong Kong by South China Printing Co.

1 3 5 7 9 10 8 6 4 2

# RHINO'S HORNS

## Michael Terry

BLOOMSBURY
CHILDREN'S
BOOKS

Rhino squinted through the glare of the fierce African sunlight. The trees and the paper dry grass shimmered in the heat.

Rhino looked at the gazelles, gnus and other animals spread out in front of him on the plain.

'Look at those horns,' Rhino said wistfully to himself.

'Curved horns, spiralled horns, thin wavy elegant horns, all such interesting shapes. I bet everyone else is so pleased with their horns. I expect they all have a good laugh at mine.'

His thoughts were interrupted by Baboon.
'Why are you looking so miserable, Rhino
old friend,' Baboon asked.
'I am fed up with my horns, Baboon.
They look so boring,' complained Rhino.

'They look great to me,' replied Baboon.
'They suit you.'

'No they don't, they look like pointed lumps of wood.'
Even saying it made Rhino feel worse. Why didn't *he*
have interesting fancy horns? he couldn't help thinking
to himself.

Baboon decided to cheer Rhino up and get him to appreciate his horns.
'Listen, Rhino, let me have a go at brightening them up for you.
Just wait here – I won't be long.'
Baboon went off to get what he needed.

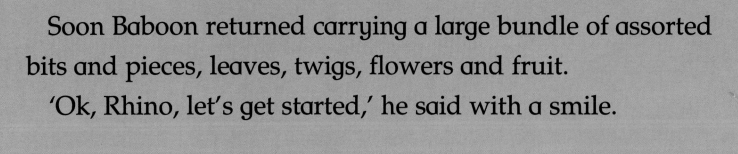

Soon Baboon returned carrying a large bundle of assorted
bits and pieces, leaves, twigs, flowers and fruit.
'Ok, Rhino, let's get started,' he said with a smile.

Half an hour later, Baboon stepped back to admire his work.
'How's that?' he asked Rhino with pride.
'No! Honestly, Baboon! That just makes me feel dizzy!'
'Really? Ok I'll try something else.'

'How's that my friend?' Baboon
asked a little later.
'No! No! Baboon!
With all those
flowers, I'll have
butterflies and bees
flying around my
head all day.'

'And this?' Baboon asked
with a small smile.
'No! No! NO! Baboon.
That's just too silly.'

'How about...?'

'STOP! I've had enough! It's not working, Baboon. And oh dear!
Gnu and his friends are coming over, I must hide.'
And saying that, Rhino stuck his head into a bush!

'Hi, Rhino!' greeted Gnu. 'Mind you don't scratch those great-looking horns of yours in that bush!'

'He's so lucky having such big strong horns,' said a gazelle. They all munched happily on the flowers, fruit and greenery that Rhino had shaken off his horns.

Gnu and the others finished eating
and wandered off to look for more to eat.

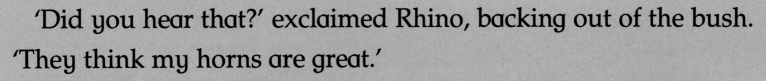

'Did you hear that?' exclaimed Rhino, backing out of the bush. 'They think my horns are great.'

'I told you so,' said Baboon.

Rhino held his head up high, proudly showing off his horns.

'See, they're not at all boring, are they old friend?' asked Baboon with a smile.

'No, Baboon, they're not,' replied Rhino and smiled happily.

# Enjoy more great picture books from Bloomsbury ...

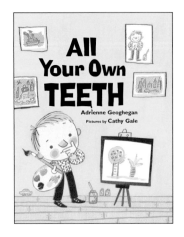

**All Your Own Teeth**
Adrienne Geoghegan &
Cathy Gale

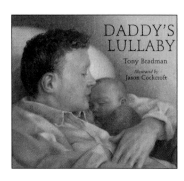

**Daddy's Lullaby**
Tony Bradman & Jason Cockcroft

**Chester's Big Surprise**
Olivia Villet

# Also illustrated by Michael Terry for Bloomsbury ...

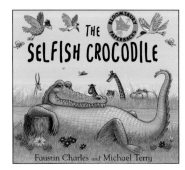

**Selfish Crocodile**
Faustin Charles & Michael Terry

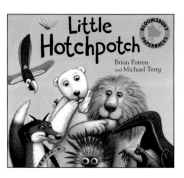

**Little Hotchpotch**
Brian Patten & Michael Terry